Dinosaurs

# Velociraptor

## Daniel Nunn

Heinemann Library
Chicago, Illinois

Customer Service 888-454-2279
Visit our website at www.heinemannraintree.com

Designed by Joanna Hinton-Malivoire
Printed and bound in China by South China Printing Co. Ltd.

11 10 09 08 07
10 9 8 7 6 5 4 3 2 1

**The Library of Congress has cataloged the first edition of this book as follows:**
Nunn, Daniel.
 Velociraptor / Daniel Nunn.
   p. cm. -- (Dinosaurs)
 Includes bibliographical references and index.
 ISBN-13: 978-1-4034-9448-1 (library binding - hardcover)
 ISBN-13: 978-1-4034-9455-9 (pbk.)
1. Velociraptor--Juvenile literature. I. Title.
 QE862.S3N866 2007
 567.912--dc22
                            2006030061

**Acknowledgements**
The publishers would like to thank the following for permission to reproduce photographs: Alamy p. 22 (blickwinkel); Corbis pp. 7 (Galen Rowell), 6, 21 (Louie Psihoyos); Getty images pp. 18, 19 and 23 (Science Faction/Louie Psihoyos); Istock Photo pp. 6 and 16 (Steve Geer); Photographers direct pp. 10 and 12 (Ottmar Bierwagen); Rex-features pp. 20 and 22 (Sipa Press).

Cover photograph of Velociraptor reproduced with permission of Istock Photo.

# Contents

# The Dinosaurs

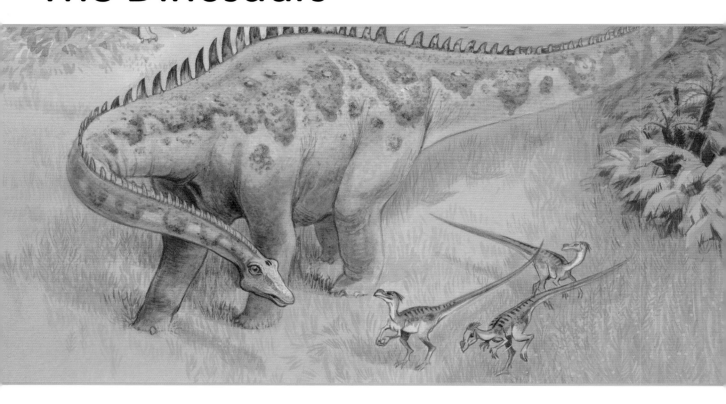

Dinosaurs were reptiles.

Dinosaurs lived long ago.

*Velociraptor* was a dinosaur.
*Velociraptor* lived long ago.

Today there are no *Velociraptor*.

# Velociraptor

Stegosaurus

Some dinosaurs were big.

But *Velociraptor* was small.

*Velociraptor* had a long tail.

*Velociraptor* was very fast.

*Velociraptor* had sharp teeth.

claw

*Velociraptor* had sharp claws.

*Velociraptor* attacked other dinosaurs.

*Velociraptor* ate other dinosaurs.

*Velociraptor* had good vision.

*Velociraptor* may have had feathers.

# How Do We Know?

Scientists have found fossils of *Velociraptor*.

Fossils are parts of animals that
lived long ago.

fossil

Fossils are in rocks.

Fossils tell us what *Velociraptor* was like.

# Fossil Quiz

A

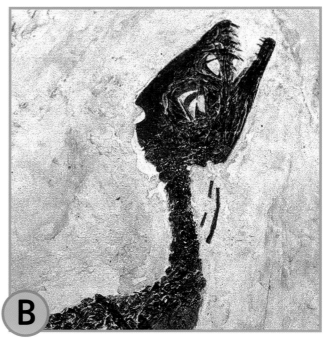

B

One of these fossils was *Velociraptor*. Can you tell which one? Turn to page 24 to find out the answer.

# Picture Glossary

 **claw** a sharp, pointy nail on the toes of some animals.

 **dinosaur** an animal that lived long ago

 **fossil** parts of a dead animal that lived long ago

 **reptile** animal that is cold-blooded. Snakes, lizards, turtles, and alligators are reptiles.

# Index

**Answer to question on page 22**
Fossil A was *Diplodocus*.
Fossil B was *Velociraptor*.

**Notes to Parents and Teachers**

This series gives a first introduction to dinosaurs. In simple language, each book explains the physical characteristics of different dinosaurs, their behavior, and how fossils have provided a key into our knowledge of dinosaurs' existence and extinction. An expert was consulted to provide both interesting and accurate content. The text has been carefully chosen with the advice of a literacy expert to ensure that beginners can read the text independently or with moderate support.

You can support children's nonfiction literacy skills by helping students use the table of contents, picture glossary, and index.